Evincepub
Publishing

EVINCEPUB PUBLISHING

Parijat Extension, Bilaspur, Chhattisgarh 495001
First Published by Evincepub Publishing 2020
Copyright © Huda Golandaz 2020
All Rights Reserved.
ISBN: 978-93-90442-30-0

Serendipity

By Huda Golandaz

Dedicated to my father.

I am the sun

and the moon

combined

For I'm either

the light or

the hope

in disguise.

Alabaster
over the edge of moonlight
is a grey stone
full of hope
and life.
My birth- wasn't pleasant, but my soul is.
Hello- I say to the moonlight
what if
what if it lost its way back home?
in the cornfields, or in the shadows of hope?
Let's say, tomorrow never comes,
once again; I'm drowned forever.
Alabaster.
over the edge of the sun
is a purple stone
full of hope
and life
my soul,
is tired
for i'm too weak
and too timid,
for a world
so peaceful,
yet
so brave.

FORGIVE

The 3 magical words

I'd say to myself

would be,

Forgive

Forgive,

and forget.

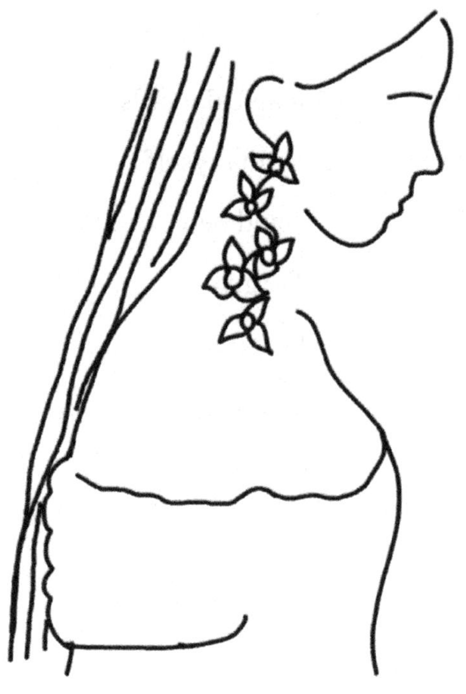

You see, there
is a light
that shines
through a
girl's eyes,
but the world
doesn't see it.
It only wishes
to see her
flaws, and yet,
unknowingly
admire them.
my flaws, are special,
they
give me strength;
they make me who I am.
I love myself,
but the world doesn't,
and
you see,
there's a light that
shines through every girl's eyes,
and the stars,
seem dull.
Every girl is beautiful.
Today,
tomorrow and
forever.

I do not care if the

sun will shine tomorrow

for all I know

is the light in me

is enough to light up the world.

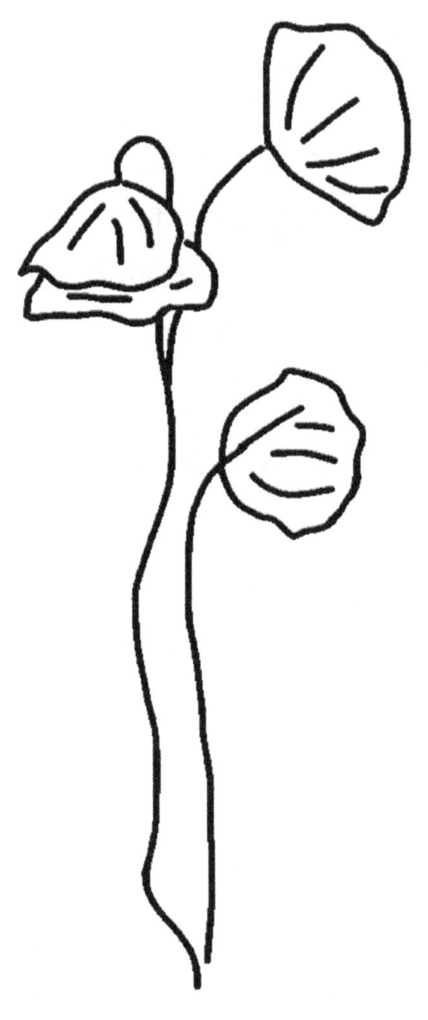

All I ever
learned from
you was to
grow flowers
instead of
thorns
Today, I might
be a different person, but
for you, I'll
always be a
leaflet
little, but
pure at heart.
I might never
say that I love you
but you know
what's in my heart
Today, I'm a
strong woman
fighting my own battles
and winning my
own storms.
Don't forget me
For I love you
Daddy.

The years-

broke me

The tears-

healed me

The fears-

saved me.

I asked my

Mother, "what is the secret to a strong woman?"

She replied,

"Every woman is strong, but the world has weak

eyes"

I said,

I love the sound of papers falling on rooftops.

I ran upstairs,

with a book and a pen

I wrote:

"One day ill be a strong woman and ill be fierce.

so the world doesn't get a chance to break my heart.

I'll be so strong

that no man ever

denies

to crave my heart

and one day

Ill be

the secret

to a strong woman,

I'll be :

a strong girl.

We could be

anything from

broken hearts

to warriors

with heavy swords,

It's just a

matter of

courage.

Whenever I sin

I recall his forgiveness

For he knows

more than my

mother knows my name

He isn't just

a presence

but all of the

strength I need.

(god)

When ache

arrives at

your doorstep;

Greet it with

a warm hug

for it came to

break you;

Use it to make you.

Some skies

Apart

our stories

began

the world

called our

name

or bought us

home

together,

we had a bond

so absurd

that the oceans would

forget their names.

In a far away

land

I asked him

the secret to

our little

story

he said words

that didn't make

any sense to me

for he loved me

and that was

enough of a secret.

Isn't it

Beautiful

How we grow

from storms

into pieces

of strength.

There's a part of me

that they'll never see

and it's not

because I

don't want

them to

It's because,

they'll crush it too.

(toxic relationships)

I was drenched
in waters and
my words
had left
somewhere from the backdoor.
Inside my house
was a big empty pool
that took all of me
in love
I wasn't afraid of the waters
but the sky made me feel some type of a way.
My hair slowly fell apart from my body
and my eyes hurt to the sound of tears
my breathing
turned rocky.
I was afraid
That maybe the waters will eat me whole
and that's when
I learned
the meaning
of it all.
(drowning in depression)

The piece of

cloth on my

head isnt

just a shield

it's my name

attached on my skin

It's my mother's lost

bangle

It's the star

in the dark

sky

it's everything, and

everywhere

I belong.

(hijab)

Blue is the colour of my soul,

Burried under these skies, I'm unknown to the world

I hope for a hand to held, but the stars have already forgotten my existence.

Somewhere under the city and it's chaos, I am remembered for the mistakes I never made.

Tell me, where shall I hide this ache?

I was never into seeing the oceans so blue, yet my soul is drenched in the blood of his coming of once love.

Tomorrow I might never see the stars shake again, or to say, shine bright again

But all I know from my learnings is that, love doesn't take much time to grow into pain.

Blue is the colour of my soul,

I am a soldier to my wars of yesterday, and the moon is my new home.

I showcase every inch of myself to the world, but the hand I held, isn't the one to stay.

Tonight, my wounds are heavy, but im yellow, and the blue is gone already.

I wore my

dress at 9

My morning tea

cups had

already said no

to the tea on their right.

By 6, I'd left the hallway

and by 8,

I was at the doorstep

by 9,

We had already met.

He was there wearing his yellow suit

and the chandeliers seemed ugly.

Tonight, we might talk or maybe

Just another glance

I hope

he sees my new dress.

There's a part

of me that

lies hidden

behind all

this chaos

It's a part

that rages

like a lion

and wakes up

like a bullet.

It's called strength.

It took years

for me to

understand the

meaning of our

love

your eyes, had

spoken a language

my heart felt too easy to catch

and I was never

afraid of the way they had spoken

For I knew

every inch of you

was meant for me.

(to you)

I wish I could

take away all

your pain,

put it in

a casket,

and bury it

away.

(to my beloved one)

His eyes had

spoken a melody

of the forests.

The birds

didn't know my name

and I

was afraid of the stars falling down

Heaven, is my home but living under the moonlight

unknown to the world.

Today,

I woke up to the sound of ashes falling

from the sky

and now

im here;

wanting to be free,

for every inch of me

has craved

the unknown.

We are miles

apart

and yet our

memories are

woven on

my skin like

the stars and the eclipse

Both share

some unseen

galaxies and some

unheard dreams.

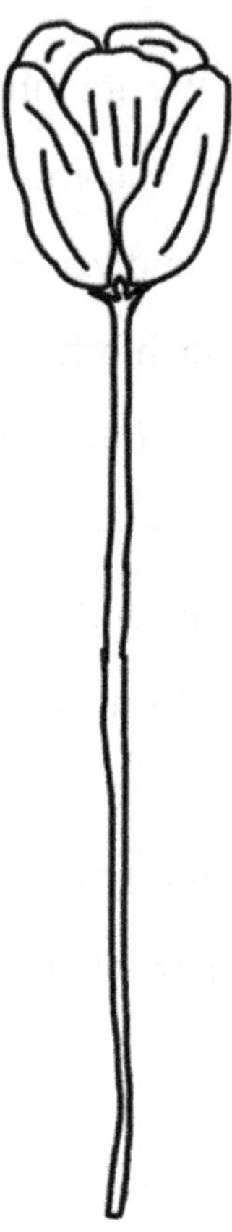

Dear stranger,

you are so

much more than

what the world

has told you

about yourself

You hold so

much power and

energy to shed all ashes

towards the ocean

you are capable

and loved by the

universe

You are you

and that's all

you need.

(a message to the reader)

When you see me

dont tell me you saw

a weak girl

who couldn't win.

Tell me

you saw a warrior

who fought all her battles

alone.

Memories
won't let you go so easily
they'll wrap you in their wander dust
making you doubt
your serenity
memories
so beloved, yet afar.
I know,
They arent a play
for someday,
they'll rise again
from the ashes
of their existence
Memories
that have died
are your lost words
somewhere buried in the sky
memories
are you
and you
are them;
they make me feel like home.

If my name had

a song,

It'd be called

"Guidance"

for in this skin,

I am all that

I need.

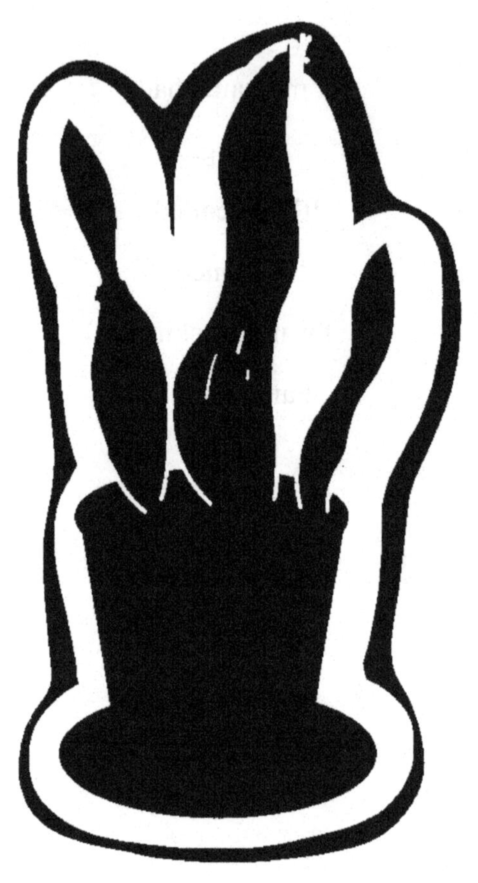

On a Saturday morning, you eat me whole

While my teacups were boiling, I couldn't hear the

sounds of birds anymore

You surrounded every inch of me whole, and you

were so invisible, yet so clear to me.

We met again on a Tuesday night, and you were

sober and brave.

My tears felt so heavy, but my arms were too weak

to carry the weight of your coming.

Over the edge, I see my life without you.

Oh so pleasant, and new.

I wish, for a matter, that you would be gone

Somewhere in the skies or somewhere near the

oceans, but you're inside me,

Raging with fire, and burning with stone

I regret the talks I've had with you.

For you've now, consumed me whole,

And I wish , you were gone, but you are inside me,

Burning with cold, taking all of me.

Tonight, I wish for you to be gone.

Oh I wish you were never even born.

(to my depression)

—YOU—

Dear father

You are so much more than what love has defined
you.

Flowers hovering above the plain grounds

with love passion and honesty.

Bright colours everywhere and attractive scenes.

My legs, wish to stand tall hoping, for more love
and kind words but

Im a prisoner in my own mind surrounded by walls
of courage, strength and dignity.

I wish to be of people that are known to be good
and happy

Who am I?

I ask myself, noticing the flowers gloom and swing
to the winds and their rhyme.

In this world filled with colours, patterns and
shapes,

Im just a girl trying to discover what it takes--to
find herself.

I am- the flower that's hovering above the plain
grounds.

Dear self,
you taught me
how to find courage
empathy and kindness
from heartbreaks
loss and destructions
you taught me
how to mold myself
Into a completely new building
made of pillars
of strength and dignity,
you taught me
how to fall in love
with all the skies and galaxies
and the storms that I hold.
you taught me
that ache isnt just a
4 letter word
standing on my doorstep,
on a Tuesday morning.
Its all that I need
to be a better me
and a better you
thank you
for teaching me so much of what i need
For if not you, I would have gone
lost searching for a me in every other soul.
(a note to self)

My words are like seashells on a sea shore

They don't belong anywhere

but they do make the earth a beautiful place.

The power a

single women

holds is

unreal

for she can

win her

battles all alone,

fight her wars all alone

and act like

they never took place

in the first place.

Sometimes the

only thing we

regret in life

is falling for

everyone and

everything but

ourselves.

Today, she

might be weak

but one day,

her eyes wont speak its mother tongue anymore

you'll see her with her flaws, flaunting and winning.

One day,

youll see her eyes and they

wont be the same anymore

they'll be bright, and full of hope

One day she'll be a women; strong, powerful and
brave.

One day, the little girl you laughed at

will be the one, you'd love.

They say, a

women needs a

man to be

happy, but all

men ever do is

break the hearts.

Today, she is strong

not because you left no

She's strong because the

strength in her; hasn't.

I read a book

about you

it said words

that didn't make any sense

it wrote about the way you spoke and lied

Today, we may be miles apart

but our stories never began.

See you were never really there

looking back

all I see, are

some dreams

dead.

There's a war
that's been
going inside
my heart.
I'm afraid I
might loose.

I pray

that your sorrows

heal

for this world

always gave you

thorns

to bleed

I know

you aren't the same

because of everything that fell your way

but I hope

now that you've grown from your storms

I pray

that you've found

your pieces

of strength.

(dear stranger)

The way you spoke

turned all the

lies to truths

I never knew

the meaning of

heartache

until I felt

your name on

my skin.

Sharp as a knife

strong as a bullet

you were nothing

but a war that

I lost.

Sorrow is within

every heart that ive met

they don't find love within themselves

they don't love their body or their face

they don't

love

they hurt

Dear mother,

you taught me how to love

thank you

for teaching me that I belong here

thank you

for teaching me not to shatter

but rise.

(a letter to my mother)

I'm writing
this letter to
you under the
moon, hoping
that someday
your flowers
will return
soon.
I know that,
my eyes are
too green to
understand the
meaning of any
colour.
When I say,
Im strong
dont splash
your waters on me
for a day may come when
it rains and
my roots will
grow stronger.
I bet you cant defeat me
For im an ocean with magic and leap.
I'm writing
this letter to
you hoping that someday our waters will join
together,
(a letter to my beloved)

My arms cover

the name of

what the world calls

sapphire moonlight.

I'm drenched in words of your coming and gone
self.

Tell me,

why do these oceans breath the same air

as my loved coming.

I'm unafraid

of the waters

drowning me whole

the fire burns its surroundings

and I melt in its presence of toxic powers

Tonight,

Im not just a lady

but a warrior, called sapphire moonlight.

He was a man

and I, a woman;

stronger,

fiercer and powerful

but he was a man

and they say,

men have power,

so do I.

We all start somewhere

from nowhere

to everywhere.

Do not touch the parts of a girl she wouldn't want
you to

for they aren't just the skin

but all of her shield.

On rooftops we sat together

talking louder than usual

my heartbeat was faster

and your lips craved the

taste of apples.

I was never into loving you

until I heard the sound of your tone

and to me

nothing was ever pleasant.

It was noon when we remembered each other's
names

and yours, seemed more than pleasant.

I never had the courage to look at those eyes,

yet they were a beauty, and

a soul, to hide.

I loved the sound of your voice

and the way you had spoken,

Nevertheless, it was noon, and we fell in love.

If my name
was buried
in the grave
it would love
the sound of
all souls
alive or dead;
my heart beats only for him
and his coming.
I know one day,
Ill meet his
eyes and
they'll be bright and
we'll be happy but
now he isn't
here and i
feel
different
For I wish his
touch and his
glance and
for once,
I wish
he wasn't just a dream.

The end.

Made in the USA
Monee, IL
07 July 2026

56552394R00059